W9-ACK-034

DISCARD

Woodbourne Library
Washington-Centerville Public Library
Centerville, Ohio

PERCY'S MUSEUM

Written by

Sara O'Leary

Illustrated by

Carmen Mok

Groundwood Books
House of Anansi Press
Toronto / Berkeley

Percy's old house was perfect.
There was always something to do,
and always someone to do it with.

His new house just isn't the same.

But at the very end of the yard, Percy
sees something that makes him curious.
It is a Percy-sized house.

Percy looks around his new yard, and he sees bees kissing flowers, ants on parade, and birds putting on air shows.

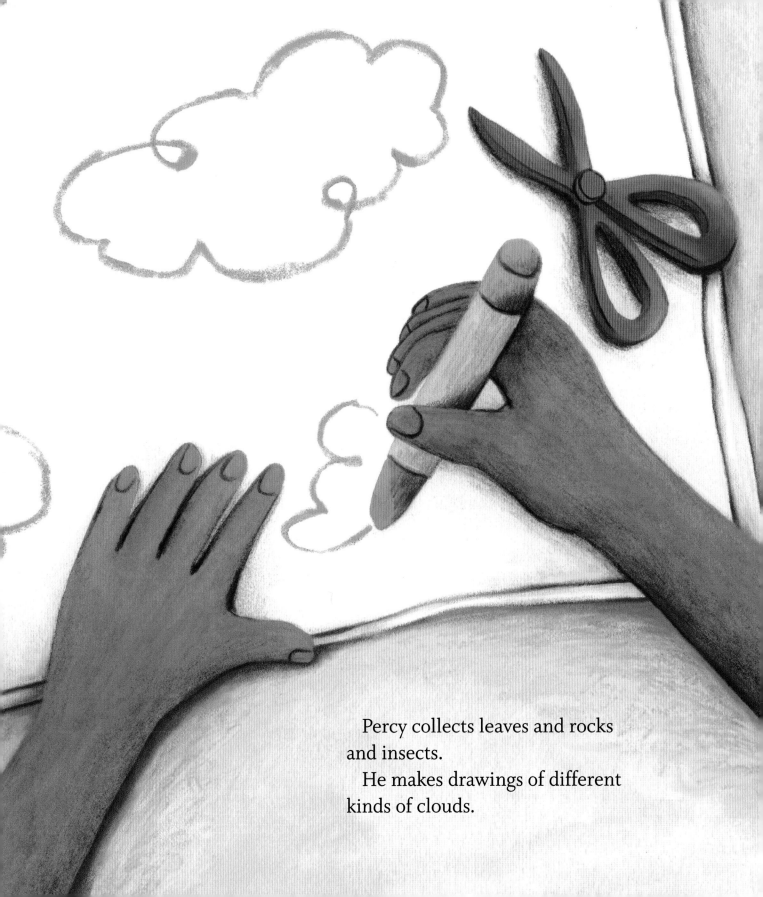

Percy collects leaves and rocks and insects.
He makes drawings of different kinds of clouds.

He learns that sometimes WILD means big and scary, and sometimes it means small and sweet.

That trees let you see the world
the way a giant would.

And that there is nothing in
the world so slippery as a fish.

Everything changes.
Flowers bloom and die.

Caterpillars become dull brown cocoons … and then colorful butterflies.

Eggs become birds.
And worms sometimes become
food for birds.

The dark can
seem empty but
really is very full.

Percy has discovered that you can be alone without being lonely.

That there is always something to do.

And that sometimes friends
can find you.

Text copyright © 2021 by Sara O'Leary
Illustrations copyright © 2021 by Carmen Mok
Published in Canada and the USA in 2021 by
Groundwood Books

All rights reserved. No part of this publication may be
reproduced, stored in a retrieval system or transmitted, in any
form or by any means, without the prior written consent of the
publisher or a license from The Canadian Copyright Licensing
Agency (Access Copyright). For an Access Copyright license,
visit www.accesscopyright.ca or call toll free to 1-800-893-5777.

Groundwood Books / House of Anansi Press
groundwoodbooks.com

Groundwood Books respectfully acknowledges that the land on
which we operate is the Traditional Territory of many Nations,
including the Anishinabeg, the Wendat and the Haudenosaunee.
It is also the Treaty Lands of the Mississaugas of the Credit.

We gratefully acknowledge for their financial support of our
publishing program the Canada Council for the Arts, the Ontario
Arts Council and the Government of Canada.

Canada Council   Conseil des Arts
for the Arts   du Canada

ONTARIO ARTS COUNCIL
CONSEIL DES ARTS DE L'ONTARIO
an Ontario government agency
un organisme du gouvernement de l'Ontario

With the participation of the Government of Canada
Avec la participation du gouvernement du Canada   Canadä

Library and Archives Canada Cataloguing in Publication
Title: Percy's museum / Sara O'Leary ; pictures by Carmen Mok.
Names: O'Leary, Sara, author. | Mok, Carmen, illustrator.
Identifiers: Canadiana (print) 20200253425 | Canadiana
(ebook) 20200253433 | ISBN 9781773062525
(hardcover) | ISBN 9781773062532 (EPUB) | ISBN
9781773063003 (Kindle)
Classification: LCC PS8579.L293 P47 2021 | DDC jC813/.54—
dc23

The illustrations were rendered in gouache and color pencil.
Design by Michael Solomon
Printed and bound in Malaysia

FSC
www.fsc.org
MIX
Paper from
responsible sources
FSC® C012700

For Daniel. So glad to have found you.
— SO'L

To my beloved brother and
sister-in-law, Chris and Chion Mok.
— CM